RESEARCH NINJA

Visit www.ninjaresearcher.com/4682 to learn how to take your research skills and book report writing to the next level!

Research

DIGITAL LITERACY TOOLS

SEARCH LIKE A PRO
Learn how to use search engines to find useful websites.

FACT OR FAKE
Discover how you can tell a trusted website from an untrustworthy resource.

TEXT DETECTIVE
Explore how to zero in on the information you need most.

SHOW YOUR WORK
Research responsibly—learn how to cite sources.

Write

DOWNLOADABLE BOOK REPORT FORMS

GET TO THE POINT
Learn how to express your main ideas.

PLAN OF ATTACK
Learn prewriting exercises and create an outline.

Further Resources

BOOKS

Buckley, James, Jr. *Never Forget: Heroes of 9/11: Canine Hero.* Minneapolis, Minn.: Bearport Publishing, 2022.

Oachs, Emily Rose. *Dog Groups: Working Dogs.* Minnetonka, Minn.: Bellwether Media, Inc., 2021.

Schuh, Mari. *Awesome Dogs: Rottweilers*. Minnetonka, Minn.: Bellwether Media, Inc., 2016.

WEBSITES

FACTSURFER

Factsurfer.com gives you a safe, fun way to find more information.

1. Go to www.factsurfer.com.
2. Enter "Rottweilers" into the search box and click
3. Select your book cover to see a list of related websites.

Glossary

aloof: distant, or not friendly.

coarse: something that feels rough.

conquer: to overcome, or take control of something.

defensive: wanting to protect or challenge.

docked: when a puppy's tail is cut short. Rottweilers often have their tails docked so they don't get injured while working.

gait: the way a person or animal walks.

mahogany: a reddish-brown wood or color.

nutrients: the right kind of food to be healthy.

pasture: to take animals out to a field of grass to eat.

socialize: to introduce a puppy to new sights, smells, and sounds so they are used to them.

veterinarian: a doctor for animals.

Index

PHOTO CREDITS

The images in this book are reproduced through the courtesy of: Jagodka/Shutterstock Images, cover; Maximillian Laschon/Shutterstock Images, p. 1 (paw prints); Jagodka/Shutterstock Images, p. 3; Rita Kochmarjova/Shutterstock Images, p. 5 (top); Eve Photography/Shutterstock Images, p. 5 (bottom); Eric Isselee/Shutterstock Images, p. 6-7; DS_93/Shutterstock Images, p. 7 (top); Bob Pool/Shutterstock Images, p. 7 (bottom); Gelpi/Shutterstock Images, p. 8 (top left); Uwe Aranas/Shutterstock Images, p. 8 (top right); Eric Isselee/Shutterstock Images, p. 8 (bottom left); Erik Lam/Shutterstock Images, p. 8 (bottom right); Krysja/Shutterstock Images, p. 9 (top); ilikeyellow/Shutterstock Images, p. 9 (bottom); Rita Kochmarjova/Shutterstock Images, p. 10 (top); Eugene Kocherva/Shutterstock Images, p. 10 (bottom); Jagodka/Shutterstock Images, p. 12 (left); Eudyptula/Shutterstock Images, p. 12 (right); Eudyptula/Shutterstock Images, p. 13; Jagodka/Shutterstock Images, p. 14-15; Rita Kochmarjova/Shutterstock Images, p. 16; Rita Kochmarjova/Shutterstock Images, p. 17; KAZLOVA IRYNA/Shutterstock Images, p. 18; Rita Kochmarjova/Shutterstock Images, p. 19 (top); Happy monkey/Shutterstock Images, p. 19 (bottom); Alberto Clemares Expósito/iStockphoto, p. 20 (top); Margo Harrison/Shutterstock Images, p. 20 (bottom); Susan Schmitz/Shutterstock Images, p. 21 (top); Shedara Weinsberg/Shutterstock Images, p. 21 (bottom); Africa Studio/Shutterstock Images, p. 22; Sinseeho/iStockphoto, p. 23; Dmitriev Mikhail/Shutterstock Images, p. 24 (top); Ekaterina43/Shutterstock Images, p. 24 (bottom left); cynoclub/Shutterstock Images, p. 24 (bottom right); Sbolotova/Shutterstock Images, p. 25 (top); Anna Tronova/Shutterstock Images, p. 25 (bottom); F16-ISO100/Shutterstock Images, p. 26 (top); Anna Hoychuk/Shutterstock Images, p. 26-27; Jagodka/Shutterstock Images, p. 31.

About the Author

Rhonda E. Nichols is a budding author. She loves to write about animals and all of their wonderful characteristics and survival techniques. Nichols has written narrative nonfiction series about animals of the deep, high fliers, and many more creatures, including man's best friend. Her best friend isn't a dog, though. It's an African dwarf frog named Max!

MY FAVORITE DOG

ROTTWEILERS

by Rhonda E. Nichols

Kaleidoscope
Minneapolis, MN

BIGFOOT BOOKS

The Quest for Discovery Never Ends

This edition first published in 2022 by Kaleidoscope Publishing, Inc.

For information regarding permission, write to
Kaleidoscope Publishing, Inc.
6012 Blue Circle Drive
Minnetonka, MN 55343

Library of Congress Control Number
2021934866

ISBN
978-1-64519-468-2 (library bound)
978-1-64519-476-7 (ebook)

Printed in the United States of America.

Bigfoot lurks within one of the images in this book. It's up to you to find him!

TABLE OF CONTENTS

Introduction

Making a Splash!

"Sit, Rodney," Beth says. She holds the stick up high, but Rodney doesn't jump. He's well trained. It's a sunny day at the lake, and Beth can't wait to show her mom what she taught Rodney.

"Look, Mom! Watch this." Beth throws the stick into the lake. "Wait, Rodney." Rodney stays seated and looks longingly at the stick. "Good boy, Rodney. And … Fetch!" Rodney is off! The sound of his powerful run thunders on the dock.
He leaps. *SPLASH!*

"Such a good boy, Rodney!" Beth says as Rodney swims for shore. His head is so big, he looks like a black bear! She gives Rodney a treat and a big hug. Beth can barely wrap her arms around him. He's sopping wet, but she doesn't care. She's proud of Rodney. They've been practicing all summer and he's become a pro. Rottweilers like Rodney are bred to learn. They want to make their owners happy.

Chapter 1

The Story of Rottweilers

A Rottweiler pulls a meat cart through the streets of Rottweil, Germany. But there is no butcher. The dog delivers on his own!

It had been years since the Roman Empire fell, and Rottweilers needed a new job. The ancient Roman Empire used to send armies all over Europe to **conquer** land. They bred Rottweilers to herd their cattle alongside the armies. After the empire fell, Rottweilers found a new home in Germany.

A woman selects a piece of meat. "Give my best to the butcher," she tells the Rottweiler as she puts money in the purse around his neck.

Rottweilers are loyal and protective dogs. The butcher can trust him. The Rottweiler will bring the cart and money back to the butcher shop and head out to herd the cattle back to **pasture**. It's a busy life, but Rottweilers love to work!

A NAME WELL-EARNED

For their good work protecting herds and butchers' money from thieves, the Germans named the breed Rottweiler Metzgerhund. It means Butcher's Dog of Rottweil.

FUN FACT

A dog that moves a herd over a long distance is called a drover.

A cattle car

A Boxer

In the 1800s, railroad cattle cars were invented. Cattle no longer had to be herded long distances. Even though trains took one of the Rottweilers' jobs, they still worked, and they continue to today. Dog breeds are put into groups. Rottweilers are in the Working Group. A few other breeds in this group include Boxers, Mastiffs, and Great Danes.

A Great Dane

A Mastiff

A military Rottweiler on duty

Rottweilers can have many different jobs. They are strong workers and loyal companions. They can be police dogs, personal protectors, service dogs, herders, search and rescue dogs, therapy dogs, military dogs, and more.

Rodney doesn't have a job other than being a loving family member. But he still looks the part of a strong worker. Even though a lot of time has passed, Rottweilers still look and act a lot like the Rottweilers that once herded for ancient armies and carted meat for butchers.

Rottweilers like to lean their big bodies on people. Some people believe they do this because they were bred to herd. Herding dogs sometimes need to use their bodies to move cattle.

Where ROTTWEILERS come from

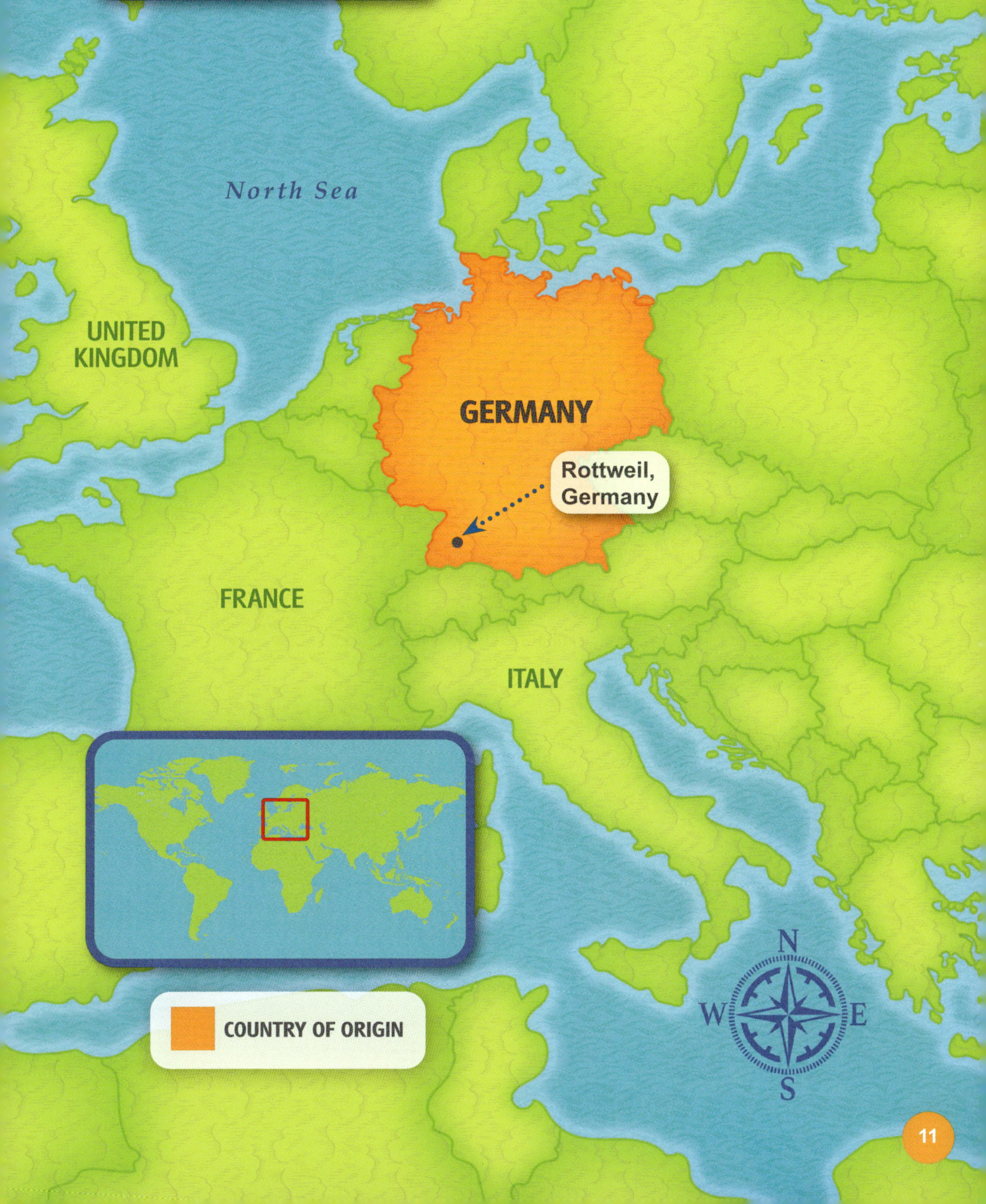

Chapter 2

Looking at a Rottweiler

Rodney's black coat shines in the sunlight, especially when it's wet from the lake. Beth thinks he's the most noble-looking dog she's ever seen. Rottweilers like Rodney have black coats with brown markings. Some of the markings are **mahogany**, while others are rust or tan.

FUN FACT
The American Kennel Club (AKC) keeps track of dog breeds. The AKC first registered Rottweilers in 1931.

Rottweilers have two markings above their eyes, two stripes on their muzzles, two triangular patches on their chests, and color on their legs and under their tails.

THE ROTTWEILER

MALES

HEIGHT:*
24-27 inches (61-69 cm)

WEIGHT:
95-135 pounds (43-61 kg)

FEMALES

HEIGHT:*
22-25 inches (56-64 cm)

WEIGHT:
80-100 pounds (36-45 kg)

**The height of a dog is measured from the top of the shoulder, not from the top of the head.*

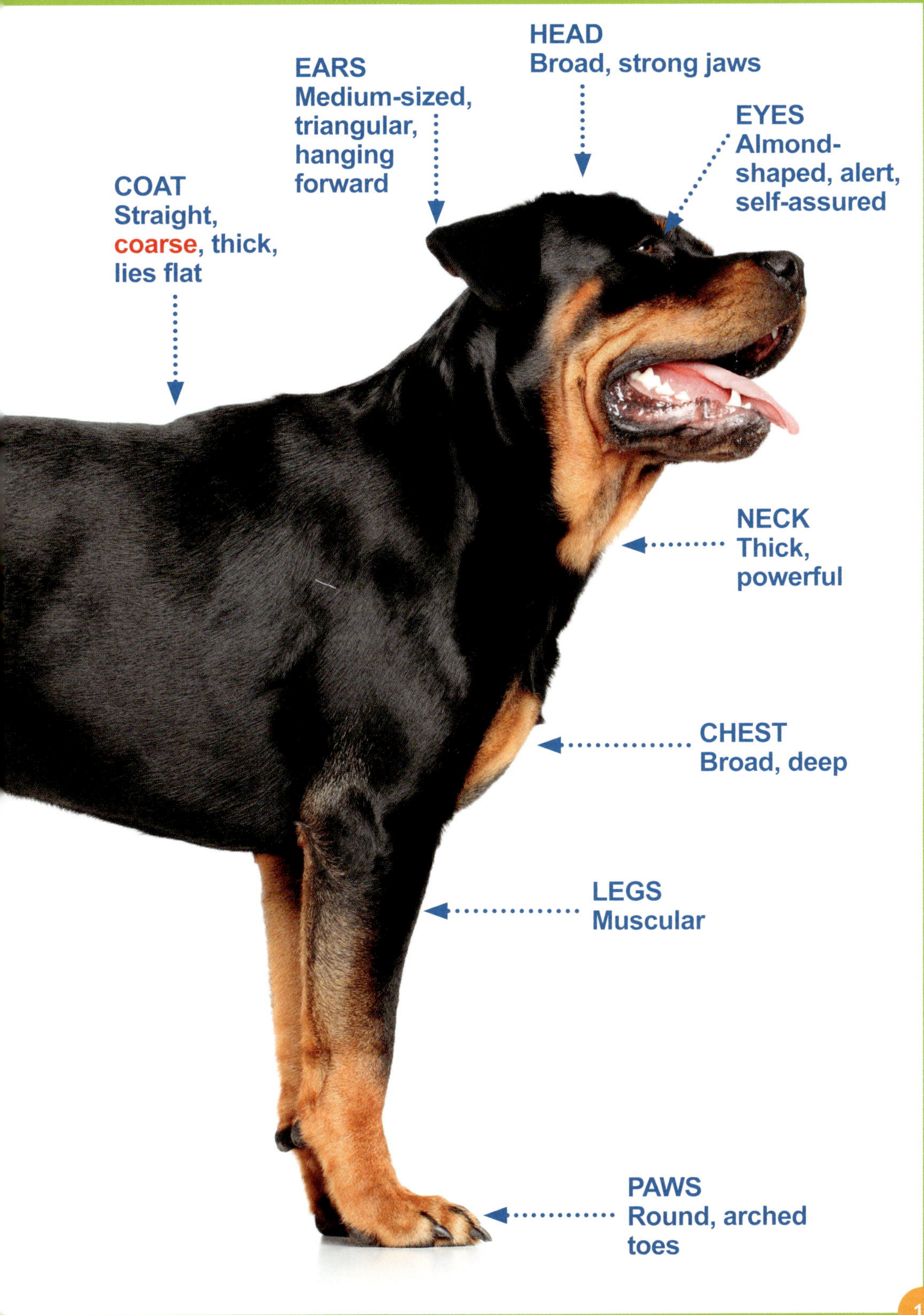
HEAD
Broad, strong jaws
EARS
Medium-sized, triangular, hanging forward
EYES
Almond-shaped, alert, self-assured
COAT
Straight, coarse, thick, lies flat
NECK
Thick, powerful
CHEST
Broad, deep
LEGS
Muscular
PAWS
Round, arched toes

"Drop. Good boy, Rodney!" Beth picks up the stick and tosses it back into the lake. Rodney waits until Beth gives the signal. He takes off like a bullet! Rottweilers are built for strength. Rodney's **gait** looks effortless as he runs onto the dock and his powerful hind legs launch him into the air. He lands in the lake with a splash! He could fetch for hours. Beth doesn't doubt he would have made a strong working dog, but she's glad he's her best puppy pal instead.

FUN FACT

Many dogs helped find people after the attacks on the World Trade Center in New York City on September 11, 2001. Rottweilers were among the heroes who saved lives.

Chapter 3

Meet a Rottweiler!

"Up, Rodney," says Beth. She and Rodney pile into the car.

Beth's mom starts the car. "Should we stop at the dog park on the way home?"

Rodney barks and Beth smiles. "Yes, please!" The car is off. Rodney sits calmly in his seat. Beth remembers their first time they went to the dog park. Rodney was only a few months old. He was so nervous he couldn't sit still. Beth had to hold him in her lap and give him a treat so he wouldn't get scared. She made it a positive experience for him. Now he's not afraid of cars. In fact, he loves car rides!

WHAT'S NEW, PUP?

What Beth did is called **socialization**. When puppies are less than three months old, it's important they learn new sights, sounds, and smells. If they have a positive experience with new things as puppies, they'll be calmer adults. Start small with things at home and family members. Then work up to public places, such as dog parks and new people.

"We're here!" Beth and Rodney run into the park. There are little dogs, big dogs, young children with balloons, and old men with canes. The wind blows in the trees, and people rollerblade and bike past them. Rodney doesn't bark. He's perfectly calm. "Good boy, Rodney." Beth is proud she socialized Rodney so well.

Rottweilers can be aloof or friendly with strangers. Either way, they need to be comfortable so they can stay calm. If they get scared, they may get defensive.

TRAINING TIP!

Dogs learn best when given treats and praise when they do something right. If they do something you don't like, ignore them. Practice commands until your dog can successfully complete the command 10 times in a row.

Chapter 4

Caring for a Rottweiler

Back home, Beth grabs the hose to fill up the bathtub for Rodney. Rottweilers can be confident guard and service dogs, but they can also be playful. Rodney trots up and tries to bite the water.

"Rodney!" Beth laughs and points the water in the air. He jumps playfully. "Silly pup." Finally, she gets him in the tub. She soaps him up with a dog shampoo recommended by the **veterinarian**. Soon, he's clean and ready for dinner.

FUN FACT

Rottweilers have a double coat. Their outer coat is medium in length and coarse. Their undercoat is on their neck and thighs and is short. The undercoat is also waterproof.

Rottweilers need their nails clipped, and their fur brushed weekly. They need to be brushed more often in the spring and fall when they shed their winter and summer coats.

Rodney jumps around as Beth fills his bowl. He can't wait to eat. Beth wants Rodney to stay healthy. She uses high-quality dog food. It is packed with the **nutrients** he needs.

When Rodney has licked the bowl clean, Beth holds up a treat. "Sit. Good boy!" Beth uses treats to train Rodney, but she knows not to give him too many. Some dogs can become overweight, and she wants Rodney to stay healthy.

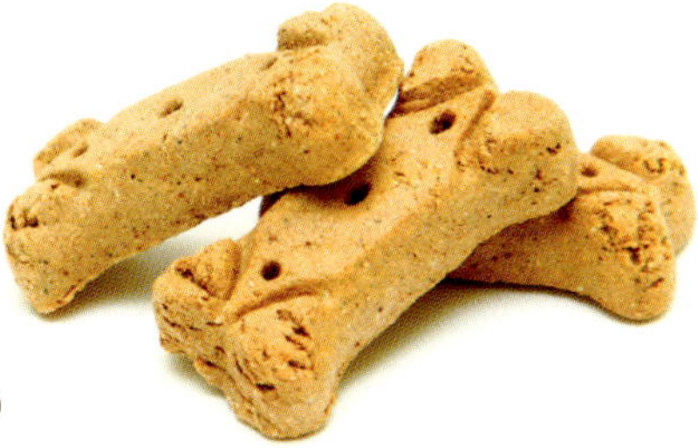

FUN FACT

Many dog breeds have nicknames. Rottweilers are often called "Rotties" or "Rotts" for short.

“Bedtime, Rodney!” Dogs need their teeth brushed just like humans do. Beth grabs the dog toothpaste. Human toothpaste would make Rodney sick. After his teeth are clean, they head to bed.

"Up," Beth says. Rodney jumps on the bed. "Such a good boy!" Beth pats his head as she slips under the covers. "I love you."

A-woo-woo, Rodney howls back. He may look fierce, but Rodney is a sweetheart. Beth is so glad to have such a great dog and friend.

BEYOND THE BOOK

After reading the book, it's time to think about what you learned. Try the following exercises to jump-start your ideas.

THINK

FIND OUT MORE. There is so much more to dig up about Rottweilers. What do you want to learn? Find out more on the American Kennel Club website. Or look for a Rottweiler club in your area. You can meet people who love them as much as you do!

CREATE

ART TIME. Can you draw a Rottweiler? Look up a cute picture and grab some markers and paper. Will your pup have a fancy hairstyle? Will it wear a fun hat? What is its favorite toy or game? Does it have a job? The sky is the limit!

SHARE

THE MORE WHO KNOW. Share what you learned about Rottweilers. Use your own words to write a paragraph. What are the main ideas of this book? What facts from the book can you use to support those ideas? Share your paragraph with a classmate. Do they have any comments or questions about Rottweilers?

GROW

HELP OUT! There are dogs near you that need care. Animal shelters can be great places to volunteer and hang out with pups. Contact a shelter near you and find out if you can help. Or can your family donate food or gear to help rescue dogs? Find out why dogs end up in shelters. Is there anything you can do to help them find homes?